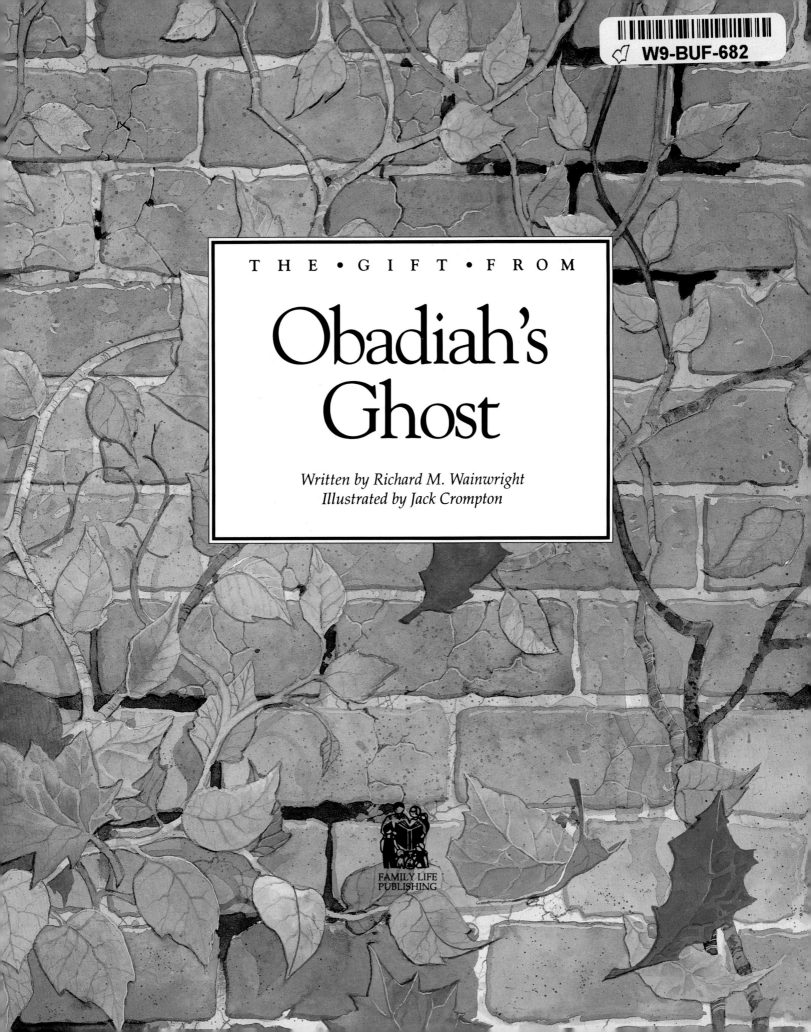

THE · GIFT · FROM

Obadiah's Ghost

Written by Richard M. Wainwright
Illustrated by Jack Crompton

FAMILY LIFE
PUBLISHING

Dedicated to All, past and present, at FLP.
R. M. W.

Dedicated to my precious children, Carrie Ann, Justin, & Nathan
J. S. C.

FAMILY LIFE
PUBLISHING

Published by Family Life Publishing
Dennis, Massachusetts 02638

Text Copyright © 1990 Richard M. Wainwright

Illustrations Copyright © 1990 Jack Crompton

Book and Jacket Design by Crompton, Ltd., Cape Cod, Massachusetts
Printed in Singapore by Tien Wah Press
Published in the United States of America 1990

Library of Congress Cataloging in Publication Data

Wainwright, Richard M.:
The Gift from Obadiah's Ghost

Summary: A young boy is helped to overcome his fear of the dark with the help of a ghost.
[1. Ghosts- Fiction. 2. Fear of the dark- Fiction]
I. Crompton, Jack, ill. II. Title. III. Title: Obadiah's Ghost.
PZ7 .W1317Gi 1990   [Fic]   89-25808

ISBN 0-9619566-2-3

THE · GIFT · FROM

Obadiah's Ghost

Written by Richard M. Wainwright
Illustrated by Jack Crompton

To: *Sarah*

May Obadiah's words remind us: With courage anything is possible!

With best wishes
Richard M. Wainwright

From: *Mom and Dad with love!*

Best Wishes —
Your friend,
Richard M Wainwright
1996

he late October sun streamed through Tommy's bedroom window. "Time to get up," his mother called on her way to the kitchen. Slowly sitting up, Tommy yawned and reached out to turn off the bedside lamp which had been on all night long. Tommy was scared of the dark. He had been for as long as he could remember. His parents had given up trying to convince Tommy there was nothing to fear. Tommy believed them, yet his fear would not let him go to sleep in the dark.

In all other respects, Tommy was a very normal boy. He went to school, had lots of friends, enjoyed sports, loved animals and liked most of his teachers. He quickly washed, dressed and gathered up his books.

"Good morning, Son," his father greeted Tommy as he entered the kitchen. "How did you sleep?"

"Fine thanks, Dad," Tommy replied. Tommy knew the yearly question would probably be asked today, as it was almost the end of October.

"Do you think you may want to go out with your friends this Halloween, Tommy?" his dad asked.

Tommy's head dropped a little lower and he sadly shook his head. "I want to ... I wish I could ... but I just can't," and a tear began to roll down Tommy's cheek.

Tommy's dad put his arm around him. "It's all right, Son, don't worry about it. We all have fears. Someday..."

But Tommy did worry. He knew his fear of the night

and darkness stopped him from doing lots of things. He hated not being able to go out with his friends at night on special occasions.

"Obadiah is back in the newspaper again along with a picture of his mansion," Tommy's dad chuckled.

Of course Tommy recognized the house as it was only a few blocks away. He passed it every day on his way to and from school. Everyone in the little town of Middleburg knew Obadiah's mansion which had stood neglected for almost 250 years. According to official records, Obadiah Smith had left an unusual will. It consisted of two pages. The first page included the date 1709, Obadiah's name and address, and stated the mansion was to remain exactly as it was on the date he died until the heirs named on page two became the owners. Page two of the will (if there ever was one) had never been found. Consequently, the home remained uncared for and empty for over two centuries.

"Time to scoot, Tommy," his mother reminded him as he finished his cereal, toast, and milk.

It was a beautiful day so Tommy could walk to school. He paused in front of Obadiah's house. The rusted iron fence covered with ivy and creeping vines still protected the old brick mansion. Some people claimed the house was haunted but Tommy didn't believe that. No lights or sounds had ever been seen or heard behind the shuttered windows. The only exceptions being the banging of shutters in the wind and the cries of a stray cat.

Tommy was thinking about what he would say to his friends when they came to his home on Halloween. It was the only unhappy time of the year for him but he simply could not overcome his fear of darkness.

After school Tommy played soccer with his friends before heading home. Again he paused in front of Obadiah's house and peered through the iron fence. He could see that it had been a beautiful brick home with a large rolling lawn and flower gardens. Now the roof and the chimneys had lost a number of their bricks. Tall weeds and scraggly bushes filled the front yard. Forlorn and lonely was a good description for Obadiah's house.

As Tommy turned to go he heard the painful meowing of a cat. Tommy peeked between the leaves of the vines but he could not see anything. The wail of the cat

6

grew louder. Tommy knew there had always been a rusty chain under the vines securing the gate. He looked again. The chain was gone. Tommy was surprised and even more surprised when he pushed the old gate and it opened smoothly allowing him to enter. The cat continued to moan. Tommy pushed aside the tall weeds and began walking toward the sounds. The cries grew louder as Tommy rounded the back corner of the house. A shed next to the house had collapsed and sticking out between the pile of weather-beaten boards was the face of a big black cat. A long heavy plank rested on the cat's back. Tommy didn't hesitate. He quickly ran to the pile and carefully began lifting off the boards. It took only a few moments to reach the now softly crying cat and he was able to free it and gently pick it up.

Immediately the cat began to purr. Tommy slowly lowered it to the ground to see if it was all right. The cat, limping slightly, circled Tommy three times and then walked towards Obadiah's house vanishing inside a partially open door.

Tommy was curious. He walked to the door expecting only to take a quick peek as he had no intention of going into a dark house. The old door swung fully open at his touch. Much to his surprise Tommy saw a brightly lit corridor. It was brighter than sunlight, yet the old oil lamps fastened to the wall were unlit. At the end of the hall the cat waited as if inviting Tommy to enter. Tommy hesitated for a moment and then began walking down the hall. Old family portraits looked down on him as he walked. Just before Tommy reached the cat it darted into a room. Tommy approached the doorway and could see it was a huge room with high ceilings. The large wall lamps were also unlit, yet the room was as bright as if he was outside on a sunny day.

"Please come in lad, I have a story to tell thee," a deep voice called. Tommy was startled and took one step backward. For some reason he wasn't really afraid, only surprised. His only real fear was darkness. He took three steps forward and entered the room.

Sitting in an old fashioned high-back chair was an old man dressed in strange looking clothes. At his feet

purred the big black cat. The old man smiled and beckoned for Tommy to sit in the other chair next to the fireplace. A fireplace without a fire. A heavy layer of dust covered everything in the room. Gigantic spider webs filled all the corners of the ceiling.

"I thank thee, Tommy, for rescuing my cat, Tobias. I knew thou wouldst. Thou lovest animals and hast no fear of them. Nor dost thou fear me even though I am Obadiah Smith."

Tommy was truly amazed. The old man's smile was kind, his voice gentle and reassuring like an old friend. He obviously knew all about Tommy. "Why you must be a ghost!" Tommy exclaimed.

The old man smiled. "Aye, Tommy," he replied, "but we prefer the term 'spirit'. I am Obadiah Smith's spirit."

"Why do you talk funny?" Tommy asked.

"'Tis a good question," Obadiah replied. "When I was living over three hundred years ago, this is how English was spoken. I believe thou canst still understand me." Tommy nodded.

"Tommy, thou and I have something in common. During my lifetime I had a dreadful fear of spiders. Not one ever hurt me, yet my fear did stop me from doing so much. I spent most of my days inside a room in this house depending on other members of my family to care for me." Obadiah paused wiping away a small tear that was rolling down his cheek. "I had opportunities to help people but

I could not overcome my fear. And it was written that I should remain here with only Tobias and friendly spiders until I helped someone learn that courage is stronger than fear." Obadiah closed his eyes and sadly shook his head. "I may be here forever."

Tommy felt awfully sorry for Obadiah. He knew how lonely his life must have been, confined to this house by his fear of spiders.

"Is this house bright so I would come in?" Tommy asked.

"Aye," Obadiah replied, "thou never wouldst have taken one step into this house if it had been even a wee bit dark."

Tommy nodded, "I'm afraid that is true."

"Be not ashamed, Tommy. Perhaps thou canst conquer thy fear of the dark. Remember there are things in the daylight as well as the dark that human beings can not see. But that is no good reason to be afraid of things we can not see. Watch."

Right before Tommy's eyes, the old man began to disappear and within a few seconds Tommy was staring at an empty chair. Tobias had disappeared too - all, that is, except a long black tail which continued to move slowly back and forth.

"I'm still here, Tommy, tis only that thou canst not see me. And thou art not afraid, art thou?"

"Yes, Obadiah, I understand," Tommy answered, "but I know if it were dark I would be afraid and run away."

Obadiah reappeared and he sadly nodded. "Aye, Tommy, I know how difficult it is and how much courage it must take to overcome a fear. Perchance I have something I can give thee which will at least allow thee to join thy friends this Halloween. Wouldst thou like that?"

Tommy smiled.

Obadiah reached into his pocket and took out a pair of glasses that looked like the eyes of a lion. "With these glasses, Tommy," Obadiah began, "the night will appear as bright as the day. The glasses will not give thee courage but when thou dost wear them there will be no such thing as darkness. Now tis time for thee to return home. Have a wonderful time on thy first Halloween. Maybe we will meet again."

Tommy placed the magic glasses carefully in his pocket, thanked Obadiah, and patted Tobias once more before turning to go.

"I'm glad you're home, Tommy," his mother exclaimed as he came through the back door. Tommy's mother was hurriedly putting on her coat. "Tommy, Julie is missing and because it will be dark soon I am going to help other parents in the neighborhood look for her."

Julie was the three year old sister of Tommy's best friend, Billy, who lived next door.

"She may have wandered into the woods behind the houses, or down the street or who knows where," Tommy's mother continued. "I know how you feel about the dark so please turn on the lights in our house and I will be home as soon as possible."

Tommy spoke softly, "I wish I could help."

Tommy's mother nodded and gave him a big hug before she left.

After taking his books to his room and turning on the lights in most of the rooms Tommy sat down at his desk. He should be out helping to look for Julie, he thought. Tommy took Obadiah's glasses from his pocket wondering if they really worked. He put them on and gingerly reached to turn off the lamp next to his bed. There was no light in his room, yet Tommy could see even better than before. Obadiah's glasses worked perfectly.

Tommy grabbed his jacket and headed for the door. Now he too could search for Julie, but where would he look first? Tommy knew the woods behind the houses well. He spent many hours exploring the little valleys and hills and the brook which wound its way slowly through the tall pines.

He quickly found the worn path which led away from the houses. Darkness had come quickly to the woods. Yet Tommy could see every tree, bush and branch which reached out across his path. He had an idea. Julie's brother and Tommy had often talked in front of Julie of the giant oak at the end of the path whose partly hollowed insides made a perfect secret meeting place.

As Tommy came to a sharp twist in the trail he spotted a small red sneaker. He knew it was Julie's. Picking it up he began to run even faster. Tommy was on the right track. The only sounds he heard were the crunch of dry leaves and the whoo-whoo of a nearby owl. As he approached the stand of large oaks the woods remained silent.

"Julie," he called, but there was no answer. Would she be where he hoped? He reached the giant oak, walked around it and there in the hollow he found a curled up, soundly sleeping little girl.

"Julie, Julie," he whispered, gently shaking her.

"Is that you, Tommy?" she stammered. "It's so dark I can't see anything."

"Yes, Julie, it's me, and it's time to go home. Everyone is looking for you and your Mom and Dad are very worried."

Julie took Tommy's hand and they began to walk slowly back along the path.

Tommy led Julie to the front door, rang the doorbell and then hurried home. He could hear the commotion Julie's appearance caused.

Tommy went quickly to his room, turned on the lamp and then took off Obadiah's glasses. Moments later, his mother rushed into the house calling his name. "Tommy, Tommy! You're a hero!" she called. "Please come downstairs."

The kitchen was jammed with adults including Julie's parents all waiting to hug and pat Tommy on the back. Tommy almost lost his breath as everyone tried to congratulate him at once.

Tommy had to tell the story three times and yawn twice before his mother suggested that Tommy needed to have something to eat and then go to bed. With a final hug from Julie's parents everyone left. His mother made him a spaghetti supper but he was so tired he couldn't eat it all. He slowly made his way to his room, put on his pajamas and quickly fell asleep with the lamp next to his bed faithfully shining.

Tommy slept well.

As he entered the kitchen the next morning both his parents were waiting. "Tommy, we're so proud of you," his father began, "for finding Julie but also for overcoming your fear of the dark."

Tommy was afraid to say anything.

"Now, don't you want to join your friends on Halloween?" his father asked.

"Yes, I guess so," Tommy hesitatingly replied, "but could I go as a lion?"

"Of course," his dad replied. "In fact, I saw a terrific lion's costume in a store window yesterday. You'll be a grrrreat lion!"

When Tommy returned home from school he found a package on his bed. It was the lion costume that his Dad had promised. He was a little scared and excited at the same time. Billy had asked Tommy again this year if he was going to go out on Halloween. When Tommy replied, "Yes, I am," Billy was really surprised.

"Great," he said, "Julie and I will come by your house and we can all go out together."

"Fine. I'll be waiting for you," Tommy had answered.

Tommy's mother arrived home from shopping and asked Tommy to come downstairs. "Have you tried on your costume yet?" she asked.

"Yes, Mom," Tommy replied, "and it fits just fine."

Tommy's mother continued, "Well then, you can help me get some apples, raisins and homemade cookies for the trick or treaters. I know you will not be here but your father and I want to be ready for the boys and girls who will come to our door."

Tommy and his mother worked together making up packages. When they had finished, Tommy's mother said, "It's getting dark. I imagine Billy and Julie will be along soon. You had better get ready."

Tommy went upstairs and slowly put on the lion's costume. Obadiah's glasses looked just like a mask. It was a comforting feeling knowing that when he stepped out into the night it would appear to him as bright as day.

"You look simply terrific!" his mother exclaimed.

"I know you will have a wonderful time."

Before Tommy could reply, the doorbell rang. His mother opened the door. There was Billy in a cowboy costume and Julie dressed as 'Dorothy' from *The Wizard of Oz*. She had her new puppy on a leash. The puppy's real name was Brewster.

Julie was bubbling over with excitement. "Hi, Tommy, do you know who I am? This is my dog, 'Toto'."

Everyone laughed. "Yes, we know who you are. You're Dorothy, and Billy and I will watch out for the Wicked Witch from the West."

Tommy's mother told them to be careful. Billy had a flashlight which Tommy realized immediately he certainly didn't need. Everything looked just as bright as the middle of the day. This is going to be fun, he thought.

Each had a paper bag with handles for the goodies. They began going to each house, ringing the bell and then talking with the parents and older children who came to greet them at the door.

Everyone loved their costumes. Billy kept moving his flashlight from side to side as they walked along the sidewalk between the houses. Tommy, of course, did not see the light from the flashlight. In fact he forgot it was even nighttime.

Brewster was behaving nicely. He pranced along wagging his tail in front of Julie. As the trio approached the final few houses on the street, a large black cat dashed out

from under a bush directly in front of Brewster. Julie was taken by surprise and before she could ask Billy or Tommy for help, Brewster had yanked the leash from her hand.

"Brewster, Brewster!" she called. "Stop! Come back!" Julie yelled.

Brewster's wagging tail quickly disappeared into the night. Up one street and down another, Tommy, Billy and Julie ran, following the sounds of Brewster's barking.

As they turned a corner, Brewster's "woofs" suddenly stopped. For a moment they heard nothing. Seconds later Brewster began barking again, but this time it was very different. Now his woofs seemed to be a cry for help.

Tommy was the first to see the big DETOUR and DANGER signs. Billy's flashlight illuminated the protective barriers. "Oh no!" Julie whispered as they carefully approached the deep excavation.

Tommy had seen men and big machines digging on his way home from school and he had stopped to watch. He remembered that he could barely see the heads of the men who were working in the hole. According to what he had heard there was at least a foot of water down there.

"Let's crawl to the edge," Tommy suggested. At the edge of the excavation the three peered into the dark.

"Down there!" Julie shouted, as Billy pointed his flashlight. Yes, there was Brewster, swimming and struggling to climb the slippery sides of the hole. Of course, he couldn't. Then Julie began to cry.

Tommy could see that Brewster needed help quickly or he might drown. "Billy," he said, "I can lower myself into the hole but you will have to reach down and take Brewster from me and then pull me out."

Tommy slid backwards slowly, holding on to Billy's hands. Julie held the flashlight. Tommy's feet hit the bottom of the hole a foot below the water level.

"I'm down," he called.

As Julie quickly swung the flashlight towards Brewster, it slipped from her fingers and tumbled down into the hole disappearing into the murky water. "Oh no, no!" Billy and Julie cried together.

Now, it was almost pitch black. The moon had gone behind a cloud. Billy and Julie couldn't see a thing.

"Can you see anything, Tommy?" Billy asked. Of course, Tommy could see just fine. "Well enough," he replied as he slowly walked toward the frightened puppy. "Come here, Brewster."

Brewster had just enough strength left to paddle

toward Tommy who scooped him up in his arms. Brewster was one happy puppy and began licking Tommy's face.

And then it happened. Brewster licked Obadiah's magic glasses so hard that they flew off Tommy's face, through the air and with a plop disappeared beneath the water.

Now Tommy couldn't see anything. It was blacker than coal. He was so scared. He wanted to scream, shout for help, run, fly, all at the same time. His legs felt weak, his heart raced, he thought he would sink and fall down.

Brewster licked his face again, and Obadiah's words returned. "With courage thou canst be stronger than thy fear." Tommy thought of Billy and Julie who were depending on him. He had to face it. He couldn't panic. He tried to breathe slower and hugged Brewster tightly. Slowly his fear began to fade.

"Are you all right, Tommy?" Billy asked.

"Yes, I think I am," Tommy replied. "I can't see you but if you reach down I'll hold Brewster up." As Tommy's eyes adjusted to the dark, he could just barely see Billy's face and outstretched hands. Billy quickly passed Brewster to Julie's waiting arms and then reached down to pull Tommy up and out.

The harvest moon popped out from behind the clouds. It was still quite dark, but sitting close together they could see quite well.

Billy noticed that Tommy had lost his lion's eyes and said, "I'm real sorry."

"Well, we saved Brewster," Tommy replied, "and that was much more important. We had better head for home."

Julie carried Brewster and Billy carried her bag of goodies. Julie thanked Tommy again before she and Billy opened their front door.

Then Tommy turned towards his home but walked on by. With the moon now shining brightly he could see very well. The shadows of the trees and houses no longer scared him. He felt that a great load had been lifted from his shoulders. He felt free from the fear which had controlled a large part of his life. A few minutes later he arrived in front of Obadiah's house. Behind the shuttered windows a bright light forced its way through the cracks and openings.

Tommy entered the yard and walked to the back of the house. The rear door was open as before. The hall corridor was lit by shining oil lamps hanging along the wall.

27

"Come in, Tommy, come in," called Obadiah. "We are having a party."

Tommy found Obadiah sitting in his favorite chair. Tobias was at his feet lapping up a big bowl of milk. Tommy was amazed. The room was now spotless: no dust, no cobwebs.

Candles burned brightly in the center of the polished oak table. The old furniture in the room sparkled.

"I'm afraid I lost your magic glasses," Tommy began. "I'm sorry, Obadiah."

Obadiah's face was happy, yet his eyes were sad. Tears came to his eyes. And in a quaking voice he said, "Aye, lad, I know thee lost them, but thou hast learned that thou truly dost not need them. Thou art a brave lad. Now thanks to thee we are both free. Tobias and I will be leaving tonight. We hope thou wilt remember us. We will never, never forget thee."

As the old man started to dry his eyes, Tommy threw his arms around Obadiah's neck. He knew Obadiah and Tobias had given him the chance to conquer his fear. "I'll never forget you either, Obadiah," Tommy whispered.

Obadiah held Tommy at arms length. "Tis time for thee to go, Tommy." Tommy smiled, picked up his Halloween bag and with a final wave headed home.

Before going to bed, Tommy told his parents of his adventures with Billy, Julie and Brewster. Of course he didn't 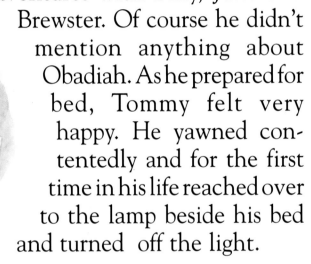 mention anything about Obadiah. As he prepared for bed, Tommy felt very happy. He yawned contentedly and for the first time in his life reached over to the lamp beside his bed and turned off the light.

The next morning, Tommy slept a little late. As he approached the kitchen he paused and heard his father exclaim, "It's unbelievable - but it's wonderful!"

"What does the newspaper say?" Tommy's mother asked.

"Well, last night," Tommy's father continued, "just after midnight, an old man dressed in peculiar clothes followed by a large black cat stopped by the newspaper office and left an envelope with the night watchman.

31

Inside the envelope was the second page to Obadiah Smith's will. This page of the will stated Obadiah's mansion was to be a gift to all the children of Middleburg to be used as a library and community center. The article also says that several people reported seeing light shining through the shutters of Obadiah's house just before midnight. Of course that is impossible."

Tommy entered the kitchen thinking of Obadiah and all that had happened. Standing behind his father he put his hand on his shoulder. "Well, Dad," he began, "Obadiah must have loved children very much to have left his home to us." And then before continuing, Tommy smiled, "but lights shining inside his mansion ...   I guess that is hard to believe!"

The
End